MEAD
PUBLIC LIBRARY

2012 Give a Gift to Mead Public Library

Donated by
Eleanor Grotbeck

In Memory of
Mr. Gus

MY NAME IS
MOOSE

MODERN LIFE THROUGH A DOG'S EYES

TO CORNELIE, PETER, NICOLA,
MEGAN, BILLY AND FLORA,
THANKS FOR MAKING
THE BLACK DOG LESS SCARY.

PUBLISHED IN THE UNITED KINGDOM IN 2011 BY

PORTICO BOOKS

10 SOUTHCOMBE STREET
LONDON
W14 0RA

AN IMPRINT OF ANOVA BOOKS COMPANY LTD

TEXT AND PHOTOGRAPHY COPYRIGHT © MARTIN USBORNE,
2011

PAGE 112 PHOTO BY TANIA DOLVERS

TYPOGRAPHY BY SUPERMUNDANE

ISBN: 9781843406266

A CIP CATALOGUE RECORD FOR THIS BOOK IS
AVAILABLE FROM THE BRITISH LIBRARY.

10 9 8 7 6 5 4 3 2 1

PRINTED AND BOUND BY: TOPPAN LEEFUNG, CHINA

THIS BOOK CAN BE ORDERED DIRECT FROM
THE PUBLISHER AT WWW.ANOVABOOKS.COM

FOR MORE INFORMATION ON MOOSE,
AND OF COURSE MARTIN, VISIT
WWW.MARTINUSBORNE.COM

MY NAME IS
MOOSE

MODERN LIFE THROUGH A DOG'S EYES

MOOSE
WITH
MARTIN USBORNE

PORTICO

MY NAME IS
MOOSE
AND I'M ONE
YEAR OLD.

ME AND MY
MASTER LIVE
IN HOXTON
WHICH IS IN
EAST LONDON.

HOXTON IS FULL OF YOUNG PEOPLE WITH INTERESTING HAIRCUTS...

JUST LIKE MINE.

LIFE IS BRILLIANT
WHEN YOU ARE JUST ONE.
YOU GET TO TRY THINGS FOR THE
FIRST TIME LIKE SNOW...

AND BROCCOLI...

AND YOUR FIRST EVER
GLOBAL RECESSION
(I DON'T ACTUALLY KNOW WHAT THAT IS...

BUT EVERYONE
SEEMS TO HAVE
MORE FREE TIME.)

MY MASTER IS CALLED MARTIN
AND HE IS A PHOTOGRAPHER.
HE ALSO HAS A LOT OF FREE TIME
AT THE MOMENT.

NO ONE IS ASKING HIM TO
TAKE PHOTOS ANYMORE.

OH DEAR,

I KNOW WHAT THAT MEANS...

MORE PICTURES
OF ME.

DON'T GET ME
WRONG, BEING A
PHOTOGRAPHER'S
DOG CAN BE
FUN,

I SUPPOSE I HAVE
TO BE LOYAL.

WHEN MARTIN IS
WAITING FOR JOBS
I LIE ON MY BACK
AND LET HIM RUB
MY EARS.
THAT'S MY

JOB. (AT LEAST
I HAVE ONE.)

BUT NOW MARTIN HAS
SO LITTLE WORK MY EARS
REALLY, REALLY HURT.
HE IS SO SAD ABOUT
EVERYTHING HE WON'T
EVEN GET OUT OF BED.

HE SAYS IT FEELS LIKE
A BLACK DOG
IS STUCK IN HIS HEAD.

WHAT?

I DON'T SEE A BLACK
DOG ANYWHERE.
THERE'S JEFFREY
THE LABRADOR BUT
HE'S DARK BROWN.
WHEN HE TRIES TO STEAL
MY STICK I GO *WOOF!*
WHY CAN'T MARTIN
JUST GO WOOF AT HIS
BLACK DOG?

WHAT'S SO
SCARY ABOUT A

BLACK

DOG?

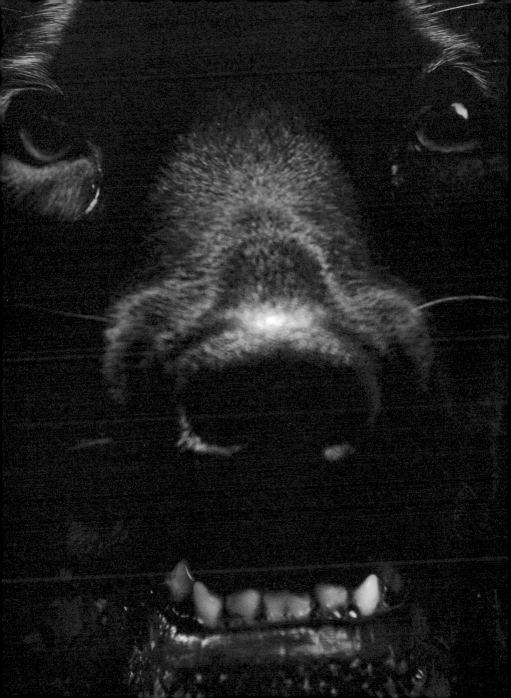

I CAN UNDERSTAND WHY MARTIN WOULD WANT TO LIE IN BED FOR AGES. BUT WHY BE SAD?

MARTIN SAYS THERE
ISN'T ENOUGH OF
ANYTHING AT THE MOMENT.

AREN'T I
ENOUGH?

I KNOW I'M NOT PERFECT.
THIS IS WHAT I'M MEANT TO LOOK LIKE.
LORD ARCHIBALD IV, BEST IN SHOW
FOR SOUTH OF ENGLAND.
HE'S AMAZING - JUST LOOK AT
HIS BOOTS!

THIS IS WHAT I LOOK LIKE -
MOOSE OF HOXTON.
MY EARS DON'T STICK UP,
MY TAIL IS FLOPPY, MY HAIRCUT
IS MESSY AND I'M
DEFINITELY
NOT A LORD.

I HAVE
A PLAN.
MAYBE IF I CAN FIND
MARTIN'S BLACK DOG
AND CHASE IT AWAY
THEN HE'LL SEE
THAT I'M A HERO...
JUST LIKE LORD ARCHIBALD.

I LOOKED IN THE PARKS...

I EVEN LOOKED
IN THE SKY...

BUT THERE WERE
NO BAD DOGS
ANYWHERE.

ONLY HECTOR.
HE'S NOT SO BAD
(JUST A BIT
MAD.)

I WAS ABOUT TO GIVE UP MY SEARCH. WHEN SOMETHING REALLY BAD HAPPENED.

I GOT HIT BY
A CAR.

A SMALL RED
CAR WAS GOING
BACKWARDS
VERY SLOWLY.
THE TYRES WENT
OVER ME —

CRRRR-

RRAA-

CCKK!

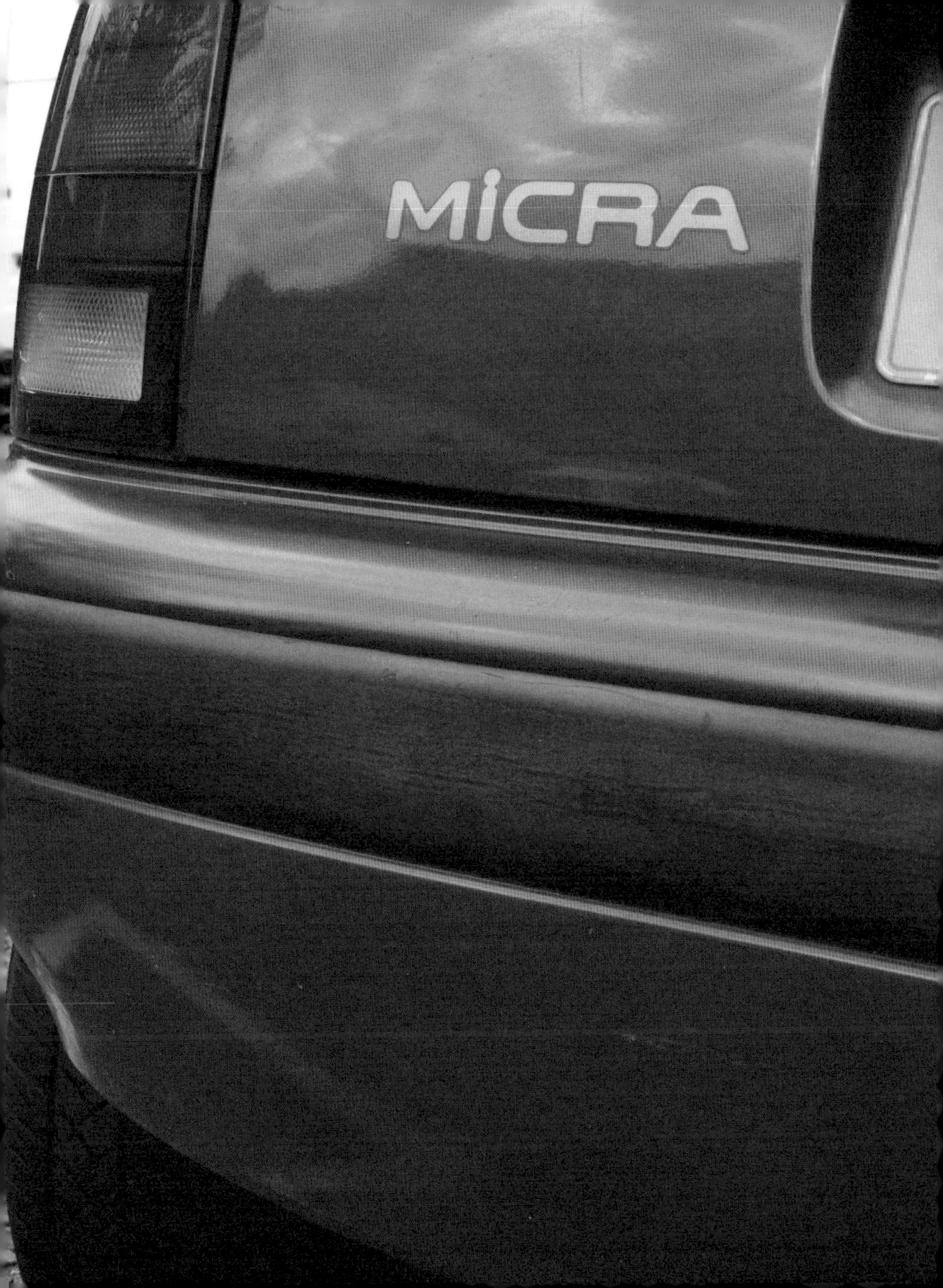
MiCRA

AS I LAY ON THE
GROUND TRYING TO BREATHE
THE SKY GOT DARKER
AND DARKER.
I THOUGHT, I'M MEANT
TO BE A HERO, I'M NOT
MEANT TO DIE...

THEN EVERYTHING
WENT BLACK.

MAYBE MARTIN'S
BLACK DOG HAD
FOUND *ME?*

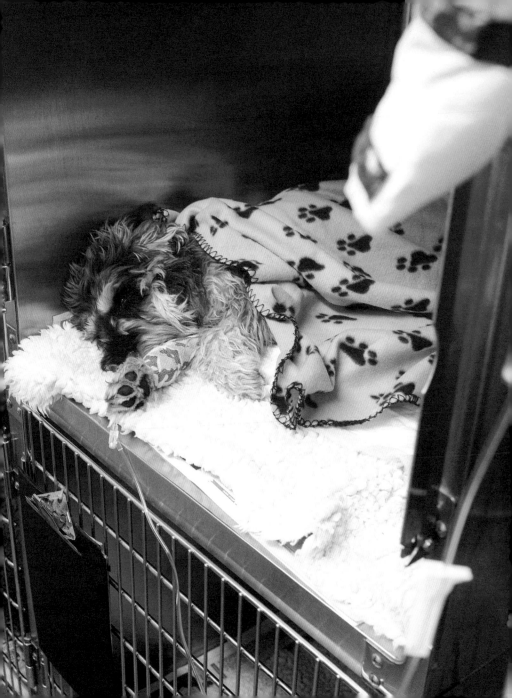

WHEN I FINALLY OPENED
MY EYES MARTIN WAS
STANDING OVER ME.
   'MOOSE, MOOSE,
   MOOSE... ARE YOU OK?'
              HE SAID.
THERE WAS A BIT
OF WATER GOING DOWN
HIS CHEEK AND THEN
I REALISED:

    THAT'S WHO I AM.

        I'M NO HERO.
        I'M JUST MOOSE,
        BUT MAYBE
        THAT IS ENOUGH.

I HAD A PICTURE TAKEN
OF MY INSIDES.
MY LUNGS WERE SQUASHED
AND MY SHOULDER
WAS BROKEN...

HERE,

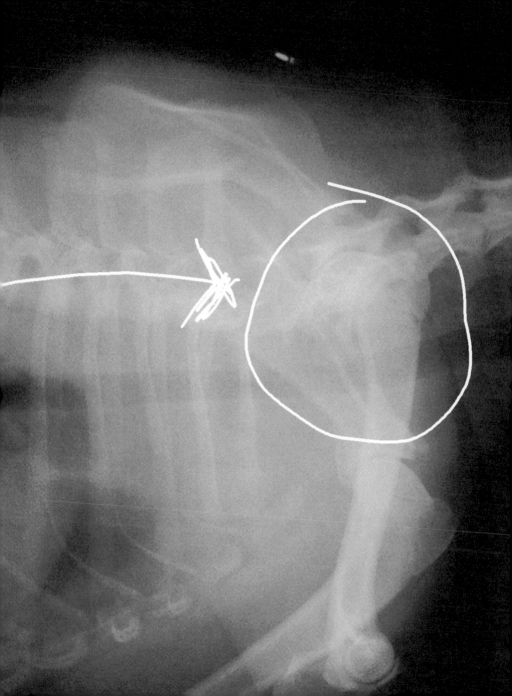

AFTER THREE DAYS I WAS
BACK ON MY FOUR LEGS.

I WASN'T ALLOWED TO
GO FOR WALKS
   BUT I COULD GO HOME.

MARTIN WAS
STILL FEELING
SAD BUT HE
TOOK ME OUT
IN HIS CAR JUST
SO I COULD GET
SOME AIR.

I WOULD LIKE TO TELL
YOU WHAT I SAW, BUT
WITH EYEBROWS THIS
LONG I COULDN'T
SEE ANYTHING...
BUT I COULD
SMELL IT ALL.

AND MY HAIRCUT
GOT EVEN MORE
MESSY.

MARTIN SEEMED HAPPiER.
HE SAID LOOKING AFTER
ME STOPPED HIM THINKING
ABOUT HIMSELF.

WHEN I WAS BETTER AGAIN
WE EVEN WENT
ON SOME LONG WALKS.
THERE WAS SO MUCH MORE
OF EVERYTHING.

LOTS OF

WOODS

TO HIDE IN.

LOTS OF
WATER
TO SPLOOSH IN...

LOTS OF
BIRDS
TO LOOK AT.,,

LOTS OF
PEOPLE
TO ADMIRE...

LOTS OF
SQUIRRELS
TO HUNT...

IN FACT
THERE WAS SO
MUCH GOOD
STUFF THAT I
ALMOST FORGOT
ALL ABOUT THE

BLACK
DOG.

UNTIL...

I SAW HIM.
HE WAS SO DARK
THAT HE HAD NO EYES.
MY BOOTS FILLED
WITH FEAR
BUT I THOUGHT,
I'M MOOSE, I MAY
HAVE MESSY HAIR
AND MAYBE I'M
NOT A LORD
BUT I AM A HERO.

SO I TOOK A DEEP BREATH
AND WITH ALL THE AIR IN
MY LITTLE LUNGS I WENT...

BUT THE BLACK DOG
WASN'T SCARED. HE RAN AT ME!

HE CHASED ME
AND CHASED ME...

AND I RAN AND RAN...

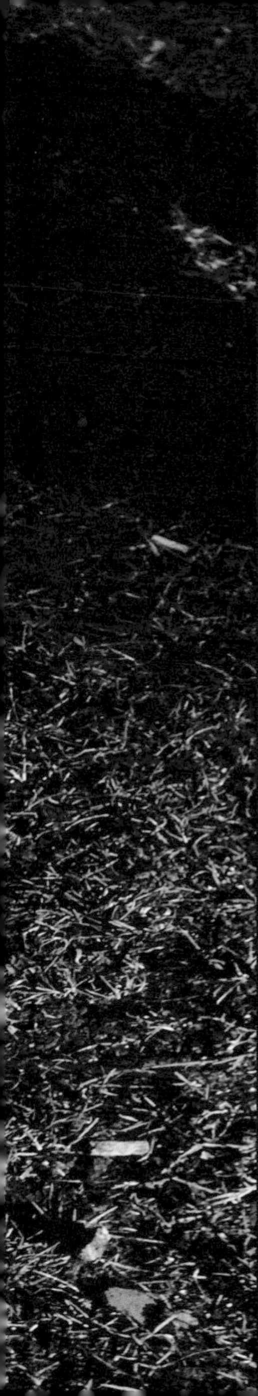

UNTIL I HAD
NO BREATH LEFT.

I SAT DOWN,
CLOSED MY EYES
AND WAITED
FOR HIM TO
EAT ME UP.

BUT HE DIDN'T.

SO I OPENED
MY EYES AND
GAVE HIM A SNIFF.
AND I REALISED
HE WASN'T
DANGEROUS...
HE JUST SMELT
REALLY BAD.

YOU SEE,
SOMETIMES LIFE
CAN STINK
BUT IT NEEDN'T
BE AS BAD AS
YOU THINK.

MAYBE A
DOG'S SMELL
IS WORSE
THAN HIS
BITE?

OOF!

THANKS

TO ALL THE PEOPLE THAT SCRATCH ME AND THAT MAN IN THE PARK WHO GAVE ME A BIT OF HIS CHICKEN SANDWICH LAST TUESDAY.

I'D ALSO LIKE TO THANK MARTIN'S BEST FRIEND HARRY FOR BEING LOVELY AND ALL THE OTHER PEOPLE WHO HELPED LIKE ANNE AND PRO AND THE NICE PEOPLE AT ANOVA LIKE KATIE AND MALCOLM WHO CHECKED MY WORK FOR MISTAKES (IT'S DIFFICULT TO TYPE WITH PAWS THIS BIG.) ALSO THANKS TO SAM AT RCW FOR SEEING HOW BRILLIANT I AM.

AND THANKS TO TONY MENDOZA FOR HIS PHOTOGRAPHY BOOK *ERNIE*. IT'S ABOUT A CAT. CAN YOU BELIEVE IT?! BUT IT'S ACTUALLY QUITE GOOD. ME AND MARTIN SORT OF STOLE THE IDEA FOR THIS BOOK FROM THAT ONE. BUT THAT'S WHAT YOU'VE GOT TO DO WHEN YOUR MASTER HAS NO TALENT.

WOOF.